GOTCHA!

by Jennifer Dussling
illustrated by John Nez

The Kane Press
New York

To Jay, Vic, and Matt for lending me their names and for
Takashi, whose name was too long.—J.D.

Acknowledgements: Our thanks to Marc Feldman, PhD (Physics, UC Berkeley), Professor,
University of Rochester; Robert V. Steiner, Department of Mathematics, Science and
Technology, Teachers College, Columbia University; and Molly McLaughlin, Teacher
Education Director, Franklin Institute Science Museum, Philadelphia, PA for helping
us make this book as accurate as possible.

Book Design/Art Direction: Edward Miller

Library of Congress Cataloging-in-Publication Data

Dussling, Jennifer.
    Gotcha! / by Jennifer Dussling ; illustrated by John Nez.
        p. cm. — (Science solves it!)
    Summary: Pete is good at playing practical jokes on his friends at camp,
but they use science to find a way to pay him back.
        ISBN 1-57565-124-6 (alk. paper)
        [1. Practical jokes—Fiction. 2. Camps—Fiction. 3. Friendship—Fiction.]
I. Nez, John A., ill. II. Title. III. Series.
    PZ7.D943Go 2003
    [E]—dc21

2002010662

10 9 8 7 6 5 4 3 2 1

First published in the United States of America in 2003 by The Kane Press.
Printed in Hong Kong.

Science Solves It! is a trademark of The Kane Press.

"Ha, ha! Gotcha!"

Peter had struck again. Peter liked to play jokes—practical jokes. And every time he did, the same words rang through Camp Lonely Pine. "Ha, ha! Gotcha!"

Even Peter's best friends, Vic, Jay, and Matt, were not safe from Peter's jokes. They were in the same cabin as Peter. And that made them easy targets.

Peter put a frog in Vic's sleeping bag.

He tied knots in Jay's pants.

He took the eight of hearts from Matt's deck of cards. Matt didn't find out for two days.

"Ha, ha! Gotcha!" Peter said after Matt had lost his sixth game in a row.

Vic and Jay and Matt didn't mind the jokes too much. After all, Peter was a good friend. When Peter's mom sent a package, Peter shared the candy four ways. Even-Steven.

When a bully was bothering Vic and Jay, Peter ran the bully's shorts up the flagpole.

And when Matt had to stay at the nurse's with poison ivy, Peter missed the bike hike to play checkers with him.

One night the boys decided to tell ghost stories. Peter turned out the lights. He turned on a flashlight and held it under his chin. It made spooky shadows on his face.

"Did you know this cabin is haunted?" Peter asked.

Vic and Jay and Matt shook their heads.

Peter went on. "It's true," he said. "Twenty years ago, a camper stayed in this cabin. He had a favorite lucky charm. He wore it every day on a chain around his neck."

Jay touched his neck nervously. He had a
favorite lucky charm, too. He wore it on a
chain around his neck everyday, too.

Peter went on with the story. "One day the
kid lost the charm by the campfire. It was
raining that night, but he went out to look
for it. He looked and looked."

Peter leaned closer. "It got colder and colder," he said. "The kid didn't know when to stop. He got sick from the rain and cold. He had a fever. The camp nurse couldn't do anything. Two days later, he died."

Vic gasped.

Jay grabbed Matt's arm.

Matt shivered a little.

Peter lowered his voice. "Some people say you can still see him on certain nights. He is looking for his charm."

Just then, the trunk next to the table slammed shut with a loud BANG.

One of the curtains in the cabin billowed
into the room. But the window was closed!

"LOOK!" Vic yelled.

Slowly, slowly, a spoon started shaking. Then it moved across the table. No one was touching it!

"Jay, the kid's charm looked like yours!" Peter said. He pointed to the charm around Jay's neck. And as he pointed, the charm rose up and lifted off Jay's chest. It hovered in the air.

"It's the ghost!" Matt cried.

Vic and Matt and Jay ran out of the cabin, screaming all the way. Peter did not follow.

Everyone waited for him outside. All they heard from the cabin was laughter.

"Ha, ha! Gotcha!" Peter yelled.

Now Vic and Matt and Jay understood that it was all a trick. But how had Peter done it? How did he make the trunk slam shut and the curtain billow and the spoon move and the chain rise up without touching them?

GOTCHA!

Peter was happy to tell them. "With a magnet," he said. "My mom sent me one in the package with the candy. It was perfect for a joke.

"I put a metal rod in the hem of the curtain and made it billow with the magnet in my hand.

"The trunk slammed shut because the edge is metal.

Magnets mostly attract metals with iron in them.

"I moved the magnet under the table. It made the spoon move, too.

"I had the magnet in my hand when I pointed to Jay's charm."

Vic and Jay and Matt had to admit this was Peter's best joke yet. But they had been really scared.

Maybe it was time to get back at Peter.

All week, Vic and Matt and Jay plotted and planned. But they didn't strike at the talent show.

They didn't strike at the marshmallow roast.

They didn't strike at the Friday dance.

They waited for Peter's favorite activity—the Finders Keepers Race.

It worked like this. Each kid was given a map and a compass and was dropped off in the woods. They all had to find their way back to camp.

Whoever made it back first got the camp trophy. Then everyone ate ice-cold watermelon cooled in the creek.

Peter had won the race two years in a row. He wanted to win this year, too! He was good with a compass. He always knew how to hold it so the arrow showed which way was North. He even knew why the arrow pointed North. Peter told Jay how it worked.

Earth is a big magnet. The arrow in a compass is a little magnet. It has a north pole and a south pole. So does Earth. The arrow's north pole is attracted to Earth's north pole.

The week before the race, Peter studied the map of the camp until he knew it inside and out. He did sprints to build his speed.

He packed and repacked his backpack with a compass and a water bottle and energy bars and bug spray and Band-Aids in case he got a blister.

On the day of the race, Peter was ready. Each camper was blindfolded and led to a different spot in the woods. At exactly two o'clock, the counselors removed all the blindfolds. The racers were off!

Peter checked his compass and his map. Then he started walking. He walked a long way. He was making good time. At this rate, he would hit the camp in fifteen minutes.

Twenty minutes passed. No camp. Peter checked the compass again. He checked the map. Then he looked around.

Wait a minute. Hadn't he passed that crooked tree half an hour ago? What was going on?

Peter looked at the compass. He turned and started west. Then he stopped. If he were heading west, why was the sun behind him? It was late afternoon. The sun should be in front of him! And the compass still said he was heading south! There must be something wrong with his compass!

Peter gave up on the compass. He trusted the map and the sun.

The sun rises in the east and sets in the west. That's how Peter knew the way back to camp.

Sunset   Noon   Sunrise

Peter stumbled into camp an hour later. The other campers had already finished. Peter was dead last.

"Ha, ha! Gotcha!"

This time, it wasn't Peter saying it. It was Vic and Matt and Jay. They clustered around Peter and slapped him on the back.

Peter was stunned. "What? YOU played a joke on ME?" he said. "How?"

"Magnets!" Vic and Matt and Jay chorused. Jay reached into Peter's backpack and pulled out Peter's magnet.

"After you told me how a compass works," Jay explained, "we did some reading. We found out a magnet can mess up a compass so that it doesn't point North. All I had to do was hide the magnet in your backpack."

When a strong magnet is near a compass, it can cause the compass needle to freeze or point in the wrong direction. Other things—such as credit cards and computers—can lose the information stored in them if a magnet is too close.

Peter broke out into a huge grin. He always liked a good joke, even when the joke was on him.

"Ha, ha!" he said. "You got me!"

Vic and Matt put their arms around Peter.
"Guess we're even now, Jay said.
"If you say so," Peter said with a big smile.

THINK LIKE A SCIENTIST

Peter thinks like a scientist—and so can you!
Scientists observe and ask questions. Then they use what
they know to predict what will most likely happen.

Look Back

On page 18, Peter tells his friends about the four tricks
he played. What are they? How do you think Peter was
able to predict that his tricks would work?

Try This!

Make a prediction.

You will need:

- paper clips
- refrigerator magnets
- a piece of paper

Draw a refrigerator on the paper. Spread a
bunch of paper clips on a table. Lay the paper
on top of the clips. Place a few magnets on
the paper. What do you predict will happen
when you pick up the paper? Try it.
Was your prediction correct?